4/8?
6/90
4/91
1/92

12/96

TUSTEN-COCHECTON LIBRARY

3 2859 00005 8512

10/93
8/94

1/95

DATE DUE

AUG 14 1996		
NOV 2 9 1996		

MAY 2 4 2000

TUSTEN-COCHECTON LIBRARY
P O Bx 129, 200 BRIDGE ST
NARROWSBURG NY 12764

Annabelle
and the
Big Slide

RITA POCOCK

GULLIVER BOOKS
HARCOURT BRACE JOVANOVICH, PUBLISHERS
San Diego   New York   London

DISCARDED

HBJ

Copyright © 1989 by Rita Pocock

All rights reserved. No part of this publication
may be reproduced or transmitted in any form or
by any means, electronic or mechanical, including
photocopy, recording, or any information storage
and retrieval system, without permission in
writing from the publisher.

Requests for permission to make copies of any
part of the work should be mailed to:
Copyrights and Permissions Department,
Harcourt Brace Jovanovich, Publishers,
Orlando, Florida 32887.

Library of Congress Cataloging-in-Publication Data
Pocock, Rita.
Annabelle and the big slide / written and illustrated by Rita Pocock.
p.   cm.
"Gulliver books."
Summary: One cold fall afternoon Annabelle finally manages to go
down the big slide in the park all by herself.
ISBN 0-15-200407-6
[1. Self-reliance — Fiction.   2. Play — Fiction.] I. Title.
PZ7.P7512An 1989
[E] — dc19   88-30069

First edition   A B C D E

The illustrations in this book were done in collage with colored pencil.
The display type was set in ITC Eras Outline by Latent Lettering, New York, New York.
The text type was set in ITC Eras Medium by Thompson Type, San Diego, California.
Printed and bound by Tien Wah Press, Singapore
Production supervision by Warren Wallerstein and Rebecca Miller Garcia
Designed by Joy Chu

for my little Antonia

One cold afternoon Annabelle
and her mommy hurried to
their favorite park.

Annabelle played under the
slide, just like she had all
summer. The big kids climbed
up the ladder...

. . .and zoomed down,
giggling and yelling.

Annabelle watched them. Then she gave her special baby a kiss.

Annabelle climbed
the tall ladder. . .

. . .very slowly and
very carefully.

Soon she was higher
than she had ever
been before.

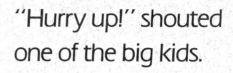

"Hurry up!" shouted
one of the big kids.

TUSTEN-COCHECTON LIBRARY
P O Bx 129, 200 BRIDGE ST
NARROWSBURG NY 12764

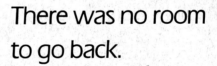

There was no room
to go back.

Annabelle took
a deep breath. . .

. . .and let go.

Down and down
she slipped and
slid and flew!

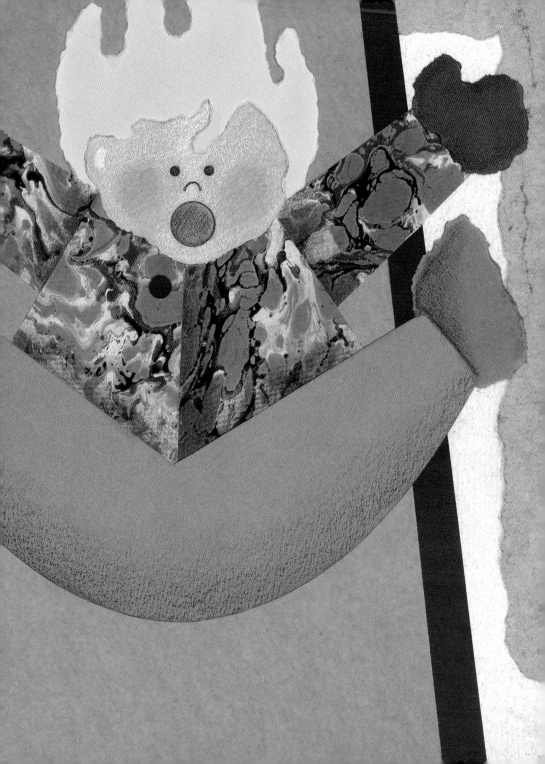

Closer and closer the ground came.
Faster and faster Annabelle sped. . .

. . .all by herself!

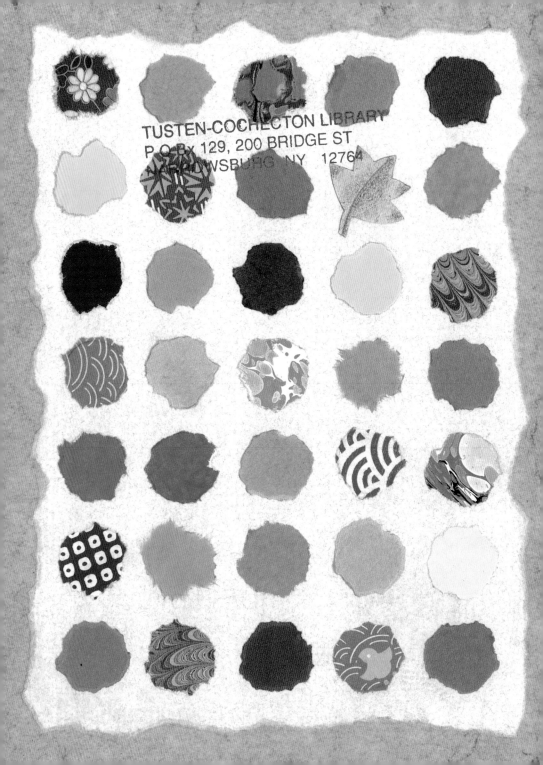

TUSTEN-COCHECTON LIBRARY
P.O. Box 129, 200 BRIDGE ST
NARROWSBURG NY 12764